RIMSHOT

RIMSHOT

Sheila G. Vestri

VANTAGE PRESS
New York

Copyright © 2009 by Sheila G. Vestri

Published by Vantage Press, Inc.
419 Park Ave. South, New York, NY 10016

Manufactured in the United States of America
ISBN: 978-0-533-16184-3

Library of Congress Catalog Card No: 2008943588

0 9 8 7 6 5 4 3 2 1

To my brother, Brian, and to everyone who has loved and lost a favorite pet.
May the memories live on.

RIMSHOT

My younger brother, Brian, didn't waste any time. As a child, whenever we took an excursion to the Oak Lawn Public Library, he would march directly up to the librarian's desk and ask, very matter-of-factly, "Do you have any books about dogs, dinosaurs or motorcycles?" Those were his three favorite topics, but his most favorite, by far, was . . . DOGS!

A stream of dogs poured into Brian's life. First came Penny, a loveable mutt named for her copper color. Sargeant, a strong-willed husky, was given to Brian by our grandpa. Blackie, a Labrador retriever, came next. When Brian brought home the next dog, our mom exclaimed, "Oh, no—not more troubles!" You guessed it; that became the name of his new dog. Troubles was a spaniel mix who could play a mean game of "catch," returning balls with her snout!

When Brian was thirty-five years old, off he went on another dog-hunting expedition. This time, he was in the market for a purebred boxer—serious stuff. In Massachusetts, he found exactly what he was looking for—a two-month-old fawn boxer puppy. It was, indeed, love at first sight. By this time, Brian had also become a professional drummer, so he named his beloved puppy "Rimshot," thinking of the rim of a drum. Rimshot was also affectionately known as "Rim," "Rimmy," "Boo," "Snooky," "Stinky" and "Pup" throughout his eventful life.

Brian and Rimshot bonded quickly. Most of that bonding took place on the couch. Rimshot learned the "sit," "lie down," and "give me your paw" commands right away. He would often generously give two paws or put one tawny paw on Brian's shoulder. He loved to play "tug-of-war" with his orange and black Harley-Davidson pull toy, one of several gifts I gave to Brian and Rimshot over the years.

Brian's home became filled with boxer pictures, towels, coasters, notepads, calendars, figurines, picture frames, ornaments and even a Christmas stocking! One Christmas, Brian's friend, Lori, dressed Rimshot in a Christmas tree skirt. Needless to say, several photos captured the moment!

We all felt Rimshot was partly human. He sometimes ate pasta from a fork and then had to have his mouth wiped so he wouldn't get tomato sauce on the furniture! He understood many words, which presented a challenge at times. Brian and Lori would have to spell r-i-d-e when they wanted to go for ice cream without Rimshot. He would indicate his displeasure with a whine whenever Brian would say it was time to go see Dr. Kathy. I especially liked it when Brian would say, "Okay, Rimshot, you watch the house," whenever he left for work.

In Rimshot's later years, he started to develop small growths on his body. He also had to have a toe removed. His hind legs started to weaken. We would sometimes have to help him stand. Sometimes Rimshot would sneak under a bed and hide. When he couldn't get himself out, he would look at us pleadingly. It was tricky to get him out from under a bed without causing him some discomfort, but I think we did a commendable job.

When Rimshot was twelve years old, he and Brian were watching television on Halloween night. Our sweet Rimmy seemed fine, but Brian sensed something was wrong. Rimshot couldn't move and his eyes looked peculiar. It was about midnight. Brian called us from Florida and told us he was going to take Rimshot to a twenty-four-hour veterinary clinic. Brian had to carry him to the van—the same van they had traveled in together when they had first relocated to Florida.

At the clinic, the doctor said Rimmy had internal problems and likely would not survive the night. Brian decided that he did not want his cherished pet to suffer any longer and asked to have some private time with Rimshot before leaving him at the clinic. Brian arrived home at three o'clock in the morning and could not go to work the next day. He had lost his best friend of twelve years.

A few days later, Brian received an e-mail from the veterinary clinic. It was a poem entitled "Rainbow Bridge" which assures a grieving pet owner that he or she will be reunited with his or her pet someday. Brian sent me this poem and said that perhaps I could give it to one of my students, who might have lost a pet, to make him or her feel better. I was very touched.

Rainbow Bridge

Just this side of heaven is a place called Rainbow Bridge.
When an animal dies that has been especially close to someone here, that pet goes
    to Rainbow Bridge.
There are meadows and hills for all our special friends so they can run and play
    together.
There is plenty of food, water, and sunshine, and our friends are warm and
    comfortable.
All of the animals, who have been ill and old are restored to health and vigor.
Those who were hurt or maimed are made whole and strong again.
Just as we remember them in our dreams of days and times gone by.
The animals are happy and content, except for one small thing.
They each miss someone very special to them who had to be left behind.
They all run and play together, but the day comes when one suddenly stops and
    looks into the distance.
His bright eyes are intent.
His eager body quivers.
Suddenly, he begins to run from the group, flying over the green grass.
His legs carry him faster and faster.
You have been spotted.
And when you and your special friend finally meet, you cling together in joyous
    reunion, never to be parted again.
The happy kisses rain upon your face.
Your hands again caress the beloved head, and you look once more into the trusting
    eyes of your pet.
So long gone from your life, but never absent from your heart.
Then you cross Rainbow Bridge together. . . .

—Author unknown

Nowadays, we often talk about getting a brindle boxer puppy someday. However, I don't think a day goes by that we don't think about Rimshot. Thoughts of him always bring a smile to my face. We have so many joyous memories of him that will remain with us forever. He enriched our lives and loved us to the very end. Just as we loved him.